MOTORBIKE BOB

PET VET
Book #1 CRANKY PAWS
Book #2 THE MARE'S TALE
Book #3 MOTORBIKE BOB
Book #4 THE PYTHON PROBLEM
Book #5 THE KITTEN'S TALE
Book #6 THE PUP'S TALE

First American Edition 2009
by Kane Miller, A Division of EDC Publishing

First published by Scholastic Australia Pty Limited in 2009
This edition published under license from Scholastic Australia Pty Limited.
Text copyright © Sally and Darrel Odgers, 2009
Interior illustrations © Janine Dawson, 2009
Cover copyright © Scholastic Australia, 2009
Cover design by Natalie Winter

Library of Congress Control Number: 2009922117
Printed and bound in the United States of America
14 15 16 17 18 19 20
ISBN: 978-1-935279-08-2

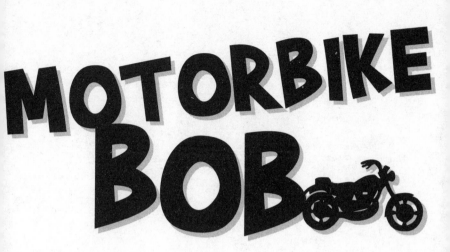

MOTORBIKE BOB

Darrel & Sally Odgers

Illustrated By Janine Dawson

Kane Miller
A DIVISION OF EDC PUBLISHING

Welcome to
Pet Vet Clinic!

My name is Trump, and Pet Vet
Clinic is where I live and work.

At Pet Vet, Dr. Jeanie looks after
sick or hurt animals from the town
of Cowfork as well as the animals
that live at nearby farms and stables.

I live with Dr. Jeanie in Cowfork
House, which is attached to the
clinic. Smaller animals come to Pet

Vet for treatment. If they are very sick, or if they need operations, they stay for a day or more in the hospital ward which is at the clinic.

In the morning, Dr. Jeanie drives out on her rounds, visiting farm animals that are too big to be brought to the clinic. We see the smaller patients in the afternoons.

It's hard work, but we love it. Dr. Jeanie says that helping animals and their people is the best job in the world.

Staff at the Pet Vet Clinic

Dr. Jeanie: The vet who lives at Cowfork House and runs Pet Vet Clinic.

Trump: Me! Dr. Jeanie's Animal Liaison Officer (A.L.O), and a Jack Russell terrier.

Davie Raymond: The Saturday helper.

Other Important Characters

Dr. Max: Dr. Jeanie's grandfather. The retired owner of Pet Vet Clinic.

Major Higgins: The visiting cat. If he doesn't know something, he can soon find out.

Whiskey. Dr. Max's cockatoo.

Patients

Motorbike Bob: A border collie, and a biker-dog.

MaP of Pet Vet Clinic

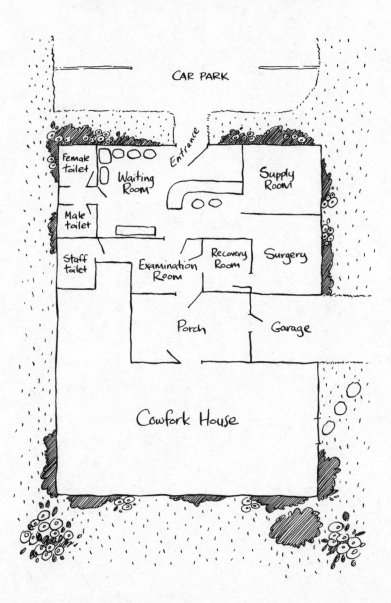

Hot Dog

"My word, it's hot," said Dr. Jeanie. She pulled a big handkerchief out of her pocket and wiped her face with it. Then she went on making notes about the patients we had to see that day.

I panted, which is one of the ways dogs keep cool. We don't sweat all over like humans. The sun was blazing down outside. I wished we could go swimming at Jeandabah Creek, but instead we had to do

Rounds. I love being Dr. Jeanie's A.L.O., but now and then it would be good to be a pet dog.

"Stop dribbling on the floor, Trump," said Dr. Jeanie, wiping her face again. "The patients don't want to step in your drool."

I pulled my tongue in and swallowed. I thought Dr. Jeanie was being hard on me. The dog patients would be panting too. I heard a soft thump out in the waiting room and padded out to look. The clinic wouldn't be open until we came back from Rounds, so I thought it was probably Major Higgins. I was right. He had just slithered through the window.

"What are you doing here?" I asked.

Higgins puffed out his whisker cushions at me. "I'm on a mission," he said. "As a major in the **clowder**, it is my duty to

> **Clowder**
> (CLOUD-er) –
> A group of cats.

discover the coolest place to rest." He surveyed the waiting room. "Shade: check. Tiled floor: check. Plentiful supply of water: check."

"That's for the patients," I said, as Higgins glided towards the water bowl.

"Very good. You may go now," said Higgins between laps. I was about to leave the clinic when it occurred to me that this was

my territory, not his. I sat down
and stared at Higgins. We terriers
are experts at staring, and after
a moment Higgins' ears began to
twitch.

"Carry on, Trump," he said. "You
are dismissed."

I stayed where I was, panting
gently. It was cooler in the waiting
room, but I was still a hot dog.

Higgins' tail tip twitched. "Stop

drooling!" he snapped.

I swallowed again. "If it bothers you, leave," I suggested. "This is *my* waiting room. You are trespassing. I am Dr. Jeanie's A.L.O., so I have a perfect right to be here."

"But not to drool on the tiles," said Higgins. He sat down and gave his fur a few licks. "Dogs are such messy creatures," he continued, spitting out a grass seed. "Always scratching and drooling."

"I only scratch when I itch, and I only drool when I'm hot or hungry," I said. Then I cocked my head. "Why aren't *you* panting?"

"Because I'm a cat." Higgins gave his fur a last preen and then rolled over on the tiles. "My system is **efficient** enough to cool itself …

given the right **environment**."

I was about to point out that his tail was in my drool when Dr. Jeanie called my name. "Got to go," I said, and left.

Efficient (ee-FISH-ent) – Works well.

Environment (en-VIR-on-ment) – The area in which something lives or works.

Dr. Jeanie was waiting for me out by the Pet Vet van. She opened the door, and I jumped up and settled on the seat. Dr. Jeanie had put a towel on the seat for me. That was just as well. Car seats get very hot in summer. I settled down and Dr.

Jeanie fastened my harness. Then she closed the van door and started the engine. It spluttered a few times, and then went quiet.

"Bother," said Dr. Jeanie. She had another try, and the Pet Vet van jolted backwards. I was glad I was wearing my harness.

I tilted my nose towards the fresh air coming in through the window. It was only open a bit, but I could smell the heat coming off the road. We drove along Dawson Street, past Cordelia Applebloom's house. My friend Dodger was standing with his front paws in a big bowl of water. I saw him put one hind paw in as well, and sit down rather suddenly as he overbalanced. I hoped he wasn't hurt. Dodger often has little accidents.

Our first stop was at Buttermilk Farm, where Dr. Jeanie had to give one of the cows an **injection**. It was too hot to stay in the van, so I went into the barn. The farm dogs, Flynn and Pammie,

Injection (in-JECT-sh'n) – Medicine given with a hollow needle.

were stretched out in the shade. I sat down beside them and waited politely to be noticed.

Flynn opened one eye. "Hello, Trump. Pammie and I are going to swim in the duck pond later. Want to come?"

"I wish I could," I said, "but Dr.

Jeanie will be back soon."

"I'm going to round up the ducks," said Pammie, wagging her tail.

Flynn yawned. "How often do I have to tell you, we round up cattle, not ducks! Anyway, it's too hot to run around."

"Trump?" Dr. Jeanie was at the van with the farmer.

I said goodbye to Flynn and Pammie and trotted back across the yard. I felt my nose drying out in the heat.

Dr. Jeanie started the van. There was a rattle, and I sneezed as an **acrid** smoke puffed out.

"That van doesn't sound

Acrid (ACK-rid) – Sour and bitter-smelling.

too good," said the farmer. "It's running rough. I think you have a little problem."

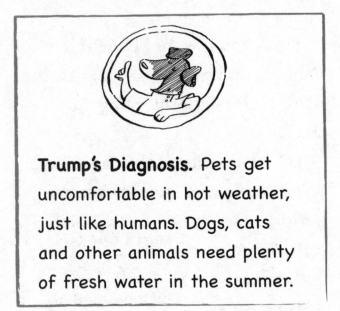

> **Service** (SER-viss) – A checkup for a motor vehicle.

"I'll get it **serviced** when I have time," said Dr. Jeanie.

Trump's Diagnosis. Pets get uncomfortable in hot weather, just like humans. Dogs, cats and other animals need plenty of fresh water in the summer.

It is very dangerous to leave an animal in a vehicle on a hot day. Even if the car is in the shade when you leave, the sun might be shining on it when you come back.

A Big Problem and a Putt-Putt

By the time we finished Rounds, our little problem had turned into a big problem. The van sounded worse, and it jerked and shuddered. I had to brace my paws to keep from slipping around.

Dr. Jeanie sighed. "This is not good, Trump. I think we need a **mechanic**.

> **Mechanic** (mek-AN-ick) – Like a vet, but for vehicles instead of animals.

We'll have to hurry, or we'll be late for the Clinic."

Instead of going straight back to Pet Vet the way we usually do after Rounds, we went to the Cowfork Garage. Jim Dooley, the mechanic, came to look at the van. He checked the sticker inside and shook his head. "This van is way past its service date, Dr. Jeanie."

"I know," said Dr. Jeanie. "I kept meaning to bring it in."

"Hmm." Jim Dooley opened the hood and poked around. "Well, you left it too late. You've blown the head gasket, as I suspected. I just hope it hasn't damaged your engine."

"The what?" asked Dr. Jeanie.

Jim grumbled, "I hope you know more about animal parts than you do about vehicles! The head gasket is an important part of your van, and it's blown. I should be able to get a new one in by Friday."

"But I need the van tomorrow!" said Dr. Jeanie. "Don't you have any gaskets in the garage?"

"Not the right sort," said Jim. "If I put the wrong sort in, it would be as much use as a cat's tail on a terrier. I'll give you a lift back to your clinic. Give me a call later. You never know, I might be able to get one sooner."

We were hotter than ever when we got back to Pet Vet. I had a good drink of water and went into the waiting room. Higgins had gone, so I had the cool tiles to myself for a few minutes. Then the patients began to arrive.

The first was my friend Dodger. He was damp and groaning. "I fell and hurt my back," he complained. "I gave a **Distress Call** but you didn't come."

> **Distress Call** – A call given by dogs or other animals when they need help or advice.

I explained that we had been out on Rounds. "I can't be in two places at once," I said.

Cordelia Applebloom patted him. "Goodness, isn't it hot?" she said. "Poor Dodger was trying to get cool when he had a little accident."

Dodger began to pant, and soon he was drooling on the floor. He wasn't the only one. There were three dog patients, and they were all feeling the heat.

After the Clinic, Dr. Jeanie telephoned the garage. She didn't look happy when she heard the news. "It's definitely Friday, Trump," she said. "Bother, bother, bother."

"What's bother, bother, bother?" asked Dr. Max. He had come in as the last patient went out, and he grinned and bent to rub my ears. "Lovely day, isn't it?"

"Lovely? It's like an oven!" said Dr. Jeanie.

"On days like this I hardly feel

my **arthritis**," explained Dr. Max. "Hot days are good for old bones. But what's

Arthritis (arth-RI-tis) – A condition that makes someone's joints ache.

your problem, Jeanie? You don't look happy."

Dr. Jeanie explained. "And *don't* say I should have had that van serviced," she added. "Jim Dooley already said it. I'll have to rent another vehicle, I suppose."

"No need for that," said Dr. Max. "Come around to the cottage. You can borrow the putt-putt. Remember? I used to use it for Rounds in the summer. Much cooler than a van." He rubbed my ears again. "It's even got a dog box on the back for Trump. I used to take old Keg with me sometimes." He shook his head. "He was a good old dog. I still miss him."

I stuck my nose into Dr. Max's hand. I know how humans miss dog and cat friends when they have to say goodbye.

"I don't know ..." said Dr. Jeanie.

"What have you got to lose?" asked Dr. Max.

We all went to the cottage where Dr. Max lives with Whiskey, the cockatoo. Whiskey was Dr. Max's A.L.O. before they both retired, and he still thinks he knows everything. He perched on Dr. Max's shoulder as we went to the shed to look at the

putt-putt.

"It's really called an Ariel motorbike," said Whiskey. "You can ride in the box on the back if you don't mind getting your feathers all ruffled."

"I don't have feathers," I pointed out. "Did *you* ever ride in it?"

"Why would I?" asked Whiskey.

"I can fly."

I sniff-sniffed around the putt-putt as Dr. Max wheeled it out. It fluttered with cobwebs and smelled of old leather and oil.

"I don't know, Grandpa," said Dr. Jeanie. "It looks a bit old."

"Nothing wrong with being old," said Dr. Max, slapping the putt-putt on the saddle. "It'll get you there. I keep it registered. I've even got gas for it." He picked up a can and took the lid off. I sneezed. It smelled terrible.

"And here's the helmet. No helmet, no bike."

Dr. Jeanie put on Dr. Max's old helmet. Then she got on the bike. The motor spluttered and caught.

"Coming up, Trump?" yelled Dr. Jeanie, above the roar. She patted the dog box on the back. I wasn't too sure about that, but I didn't want to be left behind.

"Here, girl." Dr. Max picked me up and sat me in the box. It had an old bit of blanket in it and a window cut in the side so I could look out.

It felt funny, because the whole putt-putt was shaking like a shivering dog, but I settled down, and away we puttered. I could just hear Whiskey squawking with laughter as we headed back to Pet Vet.

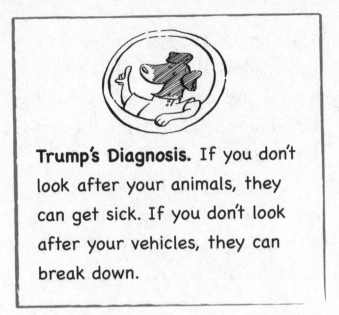

Trump's Diagnosis. If you don't look after your animals, they can get sick. If you don't look after your vehicles, they can break down.

chapter 3

MotorBike BoB

The next day was just as hot as
Dr. Jeanie and I left for Rounds.
Dr. Jeanie had wiped the cobwebs
off the putt-putt and packed the
big saddlebags with the things we
would need. I settled in the dog box
at the back.

"Let's hope nothing goes wrong
today, Trump," said Dr. Jeanie
as she put on the helmet. Then
she laughed. "This is going to
be interesting, anyway! The last

motorbike I rode was a lot newer
than this one. Sit tight. We're off to
Jeandabah Run."

To get to the Run, we decided
to go along Scholastic Street, then
out along the road past Buttermilk
Farm. I saw Flynn and Pammie
in the duck pond. They barked
a greeting and I sat up tall. By

the time we passed the turnoff to Hobson's Stables, I was enjoying myself. If I put my paws on the top of the dog box, I could poke my head out. The wind made my ears flap, and I smelled all kinds of good things.

We turned off into Kane Miller Road, and then came to the big gate at the entrance of Jeandabah Run. The Run is one of the biggest sheep farms in our area. It has an iron sign shaped like a sheep.

Dr. Jeanie slowed down, and right away I could smell real sheep. We rattled over a large **grid** and

Grid – A row of metal bars with space in between. Vehicles can cross them, but cattle and sheep won't.

into the driveway. That's when we hit trouble.

There was a rattling sound, and the engine made a loud noise. The putt-putt suddenly slowed right down and stopped. Dr. Jeanie put one foot down in a hurry, and turned it off.

The dog box was on a slant, so I jumped out. My ears felt funny from flapping in the wind, and also because the sound had stopped.

I heard Dr. Jeanie take a very long, deep breath. "I should have known better!" she said. She sounded angry, but not with me.

I cocked my head. Something had come loose from the putt-putt. Dr. Jeanie got down on her knees, and poked around. She is an expert at helping sick animals, but she is not so good at helping sick vehicles. She had black oil all over her hands when we heard a roaring behind us. I turned to look, and saw another motorbike coming along Kane Miller Road. It was much bigger and shinier than Dr. Max's old bike. A border collie was sitting on the seat behind the rider. He jumped down as the motorbike came to a stop.

"Hey there, do you need some help?" the rider asked Dr. Jeanie.

Dr. Jeanie got up. "I'm trying to get the motorbike chain back where it's supposed to be," she said. "It came off as we were going over the grid."

"No problem. I can fix that." The

rider took off his helmet and unstrapped an impressive toolbox from his bike. It reminded me of Dr. Jeanie's medical bag. He was a big boy, older than our Saturday helper Davie Raymond.

"Do you work at the Run?" he asked.

"I came to check on some sheep," said Dr. Jeanie. "I'm Jeanie Cowfork. I run Pet Vet Clinic."

"Oh, right," said the boy. "Nice to meet you, Doc. Do you get much work around here?"

"Plenty," said Dr. Jeanie. "We do large animal Rounds in the morning and the Clinic for cats and dogs and other small animals in the afternoon."

"Must be a lot of sick dogs around," said the boy. "Luckily for me, old Bob's never needed a vet in his life."

The border collie looked up at the boy and grinned when he heard his name. Then he came over to me. We both stood up straight with our tails in the air. We were on **neutral territory**, so there was no reason for either of us to ask permission or to **submit**.

I said, "I'm Trump, Dr. Jeanie's A.L.O. That's an Animal Liaison Officer.

Neutral territory (NEWT-ral TERR-i-tory) – Territory that doesn't belong to either of you.

Submit – When dogs meet, the one in the weaker position submits, or admits the other dog is the boss.

I help to make the patients feel comfortable."

"I'm Motorbike Bob," said the border collie. He sat down and held up a paw. "Always pleased to meet another biker-dog, Trump. There's nothing like the feel of wind in your ears, right?"

I explained that I didn't always ride on the back of a motorbike. "The Pet Vet van broke down, so we borrowed this putt-putt."

Bob grinned again, lolling his tongue sideways. I saw he had very clean teeth. "That explains the dog box! *Real* biker-dogs can balance without one." He twirled in a circle. "Like me."

"You could fall and get hurt if

something goes wrong with the bike," I said.

"I never fall. I'd just jump clear. You were unlucky to lose your chain. But never mind. Greg will fix it. Greg can do anything." He wagged his tail and lifted his eyebrows. "Want to come for a run up the hill while we wait for them?"

"Not now," I said.

"I thought terriers were always ready for a run?"

"If I just run off, Dr. Jeanie will be worried. We have to get Rounds done."

"Greg never worries. He knows I can look after myself," said Bob. "We could herd the sheep a bit. That's always fun."

"I'm not a herding dog. I'm an A.L.O.," I said.

Bob got down on his elbows and hitched his eyebrows up again. "Aw, come on, Trump! Loosen up!"

I looked at Dr. Jeanie. She was still talking to Bob's person, but I gave a little whine.

"Off you go, then," she said, smiling at me. "But don't go far."

Bob swept his tail in a circle, and bounced up. I darted at him and pretended to snap at his tail. Bob jumped sideways over a thistle, and I scooted around it. We had a fine game of set-and-dash.

"I used to play this with my brother and sisters!" I told Bob. "There's not as much time for games

now."

"There's *always* time for games,"
said Bob. He bowled me over with
his snout.

I was trying to bowl *him* over when
Dr. Jeanie called. "Trump! Time to go!"

"Your person has fixed the
putt-putt," I said. "Dr. Jeanie and I
can get on with our work."

"Told you Greg would fix it," said Bob. "Greg can fix anything. Thanks for the game. It was fun. See you around, Trump?"

"You will, next time you come to Pet Vet Clinic," I said.

"Ha! That'll be never!" Motorbike Bob chased his tail in a circle. "A healthy dog never needs to visit a vet. It's just a matter of eating plenty and getting enough exercise. I always keep busy."

Greg put on his helmet. "All done," he said, "but it needs a new chain and sprockets. These are beyond attention. They're all pretty well worn. You don't want this happening again." He started up his bike. Bob sprang up behind him.

"Bye, Trump!" said Bob, and they roared away.

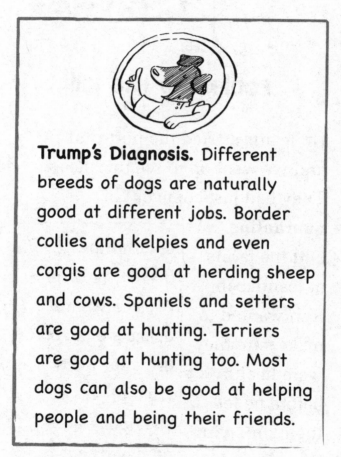

Trump's Diagnosis. Different breeds of dogs are naturally good at different jobs. Border collies and kelpies and even corgis are good at herding sheep and cows. Spaniels and setters are good at hunting. Terriers are good at hunting too. Most dogs can also be good at helping people and being their friends.

Chapter 4

Ponies on the Hill

Dr. Jeanie started the putt-putt, and we went on to see the sheep. They had just come out of **quarantine** and the farmer at Jeandabah Run wanted to make sure they were healthy before he let them mix with the others. If

> **Quarantine** (KWOR-n-teen) – A place where animals or people are kept away from others so they don't pass on any diseases.

one sick sheep gets mixed in with healthy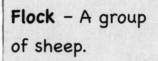

Flock – A group of sheep.

ones, the whole **flock** can get sick.

They were big, woolly sheep called Merinos. They milled around while Dr. Jeanie inspected them.

I trotted with her, but the sheep ignored me. They are used to kelpies, or border collies like Motorbike Bob. Sheep don't care about terriers.

When Dr. Jeanie had finished with the sheep, she told the farmer how Greg had fixed the putt-putt. "Do you know him?" she asked. "He was very helpful, and a good mechanic."

"Can't say I do," said the farmer.

"Maybe he was just passing through."

"Maybe," said Dr. Jeanie. "He did ask if I worked at the Run, though. That's what the locals call this place, isn't it?"

The farmer shrugged. "He might be visiting someone nearby. It's just as well you met him, anyway. I can fix my old tractor, but I've never been bothered with bikes." He grinned. "Especially an old one like this. Where did you find it?"

"It belongs to Dr. Max," said Dr. Jeanie. She turned back to the sheep. "You can go ahead and put these out with the others. Come on, Trump." She clicked her fingers. This time, I jumped up into the dog box myself.

We had one more call to make before we finished Rounds, to some ponies with sore eyes. They belonged to Carla Lother, who runs the Elias Hill Pony Stud. The road up the hill is narrow and winding, and quite steep. There are gullies on either side. At least it was cooler as we went in and out of patches of shade. Sometimes, the trees on either side of the road almost met overhead. It would have been peaceful if the motor hadn't been making my ears feel funny. I crouched down inside the dog box, and sneezed.

Then I sniffed and sneezed again. There was a bit of smoke in the air. That wasn't unusual in the summer.

Sometimes people are silly enough
to let grass or trees catch on fire.
I hoped it was a long way off.

When we stopped at the top of
the hill, I could already smell hot
ponies. I jumped out and gave my
head a good shake, then turned
to the sick animals. Carla Lother,
the owner, had shut them in a
yard. They were shuffling around
uneasily, so I trotted up to the fence,

and introduced myself.

"You're a small dog," said one of them. Ponies often say obvious things. This one was black, and its eyes looked sore and runny. "Are you going to chase us?"

"No, I'm an A.L.O.," I said. "Dr. Jeanie has come to make you feel better, so just keep calm while she examines you. Have you all got sore eyes?"

"Yes," said the black pony. She shook her head, and rubbed her eye on her knee. "It hurts and it itches, and the flies won't go away."

I noticed they were all shaking their heads, and swishing their long tails. There were a lot of flies buzzing around, and I snapped at a few that wanted to land on me.

"I even put my face in the water trough to get rid of them," said a grey pony. "They just come back, though."

I looked them over. Apart from their sore eyes, they all seemed healthy. That was a good thing. Sometimes, animals have more than one thing wrong with them, especially if they are not well looked after.

Dr. Jeanie asked Carla to hold one of the ponies steady while she examined its eyes. Carla took the black one by the **halter** and

Halter (HOLL-ter) – A leather or rope collar that fits around a horse's head and over its nose.

held it firmly. Dr. Jeanie put on gloves and checked the sore eyes. The pony flinched.

"It itches and hurts!" she complained, and snorted.

"Dr. Jeanie will help," I said again. "It will be quicker if you keep calm."

Dr. Jeanie nodded to Carla

Conjunctivitis (con–JUNCT–iv–eye–tis) – An eye disease that inflames the conjunctiva, which is part of the eye.

to let the pony go. "It's **conjunctivitis**," she said. "Some people call it pink eye. It's a nasty infection and hot weather makes it worse. The flies have been spreading it from one pony to another."

"I wondered about that," said Carla. She pushed her hands into the pockets of her jeans. "Should your dog be so close to the ponies?"

"Trump is fine with other animals," said Dr. Jeanie. "She knows enough not to get trodden on or kicked, and she's really good at calming them down if they're nervous."

Dr. Jeanie went to the putt-putt and opened her saddlebag. "You need to bathe the eyes and put this ointment in," she said. "You could also use some fly repellent. It might help if you put the ponies in the stable during the heat of the day, but you'll have to disinfect the mangers and walls afterwards if you do. It's very contagious. Oh, and wash your hands well after you handle the infected ones."

Carla sighed. "I'll need a lot of ointment to treat them all. And I suppose the ones in the other paddock will come down with it too?"

"Probably," said Dr. Jeanie. "You can catch it early, though," she added, as she showed Carla how to administer the ointment.

"It stings!" said the black pony. "My eyes are all blurry."

"It will make you better," I said. "Just try not to rub at it."

The pony snorted, but she did calm down. Ponies are herd animals. If one is calm the others usually settle too.

Dr. Jeanie put her gloves in a bag for disposal and washed her hands under the tap by the fence. "The ointment will work quickly," she said. "Just stay alert in case it recurs. Is there anyone to help you?"

"My brother Greg will help. He's coming to stay with me for a couple of weeks while he waits to start a new job," said Carla. She looked at her watch. "He should have been here by now. He called ages ago to tell me he was on his way." She sighed. "He's usually reliable."

Trump's Diagnosis. Flies and other insects spread a lot of diseases. If your pet has any sores or if its eyes are running you should do your best to keep the flies away. You can get special fly repellent to use on animals.

Chapter 5

Distress Call

"Your brother Greg," said Dr. Jeanie. "Would he be riding a motorbike, with a border collie on the back?"

"That's right," said Carla. "Motorbike Bob loves to ride on the back of the saddle. I'm always afraid he'll fall off, but he never does." She took the ointment from Dr. Jeanie. "How do you know Greg? He lives up past Doggeroo. Have you seen him today?"

"We met him this morning near Jeandabah Run," said Dr. Jeanie. "In fact, he helped me out of a problem." She explained how Greg had fixed the putt-putt.

Carla laughed. "Greg's good at fixing things, and he's always ready to help."

I remembered that Motorbike Bob had said the same thing.

Dr. Jeanie said she would come back to see the ponies in a few days, and I jumped back into the dog box. She kicked the starter and off we went. As we left Carla's place, I wondered where Greg and Motorbike Bob were. Surely they should have reached Elias Hill *before* Dr. Jeanie and me? We had spent some time at Jeandabah Run, and Greg's bike was bigger and faster than the putt-putt. I stuck my head over the edge of the dog box, but the wind in my nose made me sneeze. I sat down again. What Greg and Motorbike Bob did was none of my business. Bob was a friendly dog, and we'd had a good game, but he was not our patient.

Dr. Jeanie was riding quite slowly, because the hill was steep, and the road twisted and turned. There were also large stones on it, and she was being careful not to hit them. I could smell the trees and hot grass, and the scent of the ponies still reached my nose. I snuffed the air. I smelled the sheep at the Run, and even some cows somewhere. Then I sneezed. There was that whiff of smoke again. It was coming from somewhere in the deep gully.

We were about halfway down the hill when I heard a Distress Call. It was a single, loud yelp.

I stiffened. Dogs bark for all kinds of reasons. Sometimes, it's just for something to do. Distress Calls are different. They are only used if something is wrong.

I got up on my hind legs and listened. It was difficult to hear much over the putt-putt's engine. I knew Dr. Jeanie would not hear the call. She is a human and I am a terrier, so my hearing is much better than hers. The Distress Call came again. There was only one thing to do. I jumped out of the dog box. If Dr. Jeanie had been riding fast, I would have been hurt, but I landed safely on the grass at the side of the road. Dr. Jeanie and the putt-putt went on down the hill. I wanted to run after her, but I gave myself a lecture.

"Trump, you are an A.L.O. You

heard a Distress Call and it is your duty to respond. Dr. Jeanie will miss you soon. Then she will come back for you."

I hoped it wouldn't take too long.

I pricked up my ears and listened. The yelp came again, and I could tell it was coming from part way down the gully. I trotted back up the road and sniffed the air. I could still smell hot trees and a trace of smoke, but I could also smell another dog. I knew that scent. It wasn't Dodger or Flynn or Pammie or any of my friends. It was Motorbike Bob, the border collie.

"Bob!" I barked. "Bob! I hear you. If you are hurt, stay where you are."

I turned off the road and started

down the slope under the trees.
Then I smelled blood.

"Bob! Bob!" I barked. There was
silence, and then I heard a whine
and a rustling sound. I ran down
the slope towards the sound. Bob
was lying on the ground. He seemed
to have fallen over, and I soon saw
why. He had a deep cut across his
paw. It was bleeding a lot. When
Bob saw me, he tried to get up.

"Trump ... I have to –"

"You have to keep still," I said
firmly. I sniffed at his bleeding
paw. If it had been a small wound I
would have told him to lick it clean,
and limp back to the road on three
legs, but this was serious. He was
weak and dehydrated.

"I have to get up." He kicked his hind paws and churned his tail, but he was too weak.

I was very worried. As Dr. Jeanie's A.L.O. I had helped a lot of sick, frightened animals to feel calmer, but Dr. Jeanie had been with me then. This was not a little problem that an A.L.O. could solve. This was a big

one that needed a vet. I had to think
of something quickly.

Trump's Diagnosis. If animals or
people are injured, they can get
weak if they lose too much blood.
Vets or human doctors can stop
the bleeding. Sometimes they
have to give a patient some more
blood. This is called a transfusion.

chapter 6

Trump to the Rescue

"Keep very still and very calm," I told Bob.

"I have to get help for Greg. Greg will fix it."

I sniffed the air. "Where *is* Greg?"

"I need to help him."

"You need Dr. Jeanie," I said firmly. "I will get her to come to you, but you have to stay still."

"I have to find Greg."

I sighed. This conversation was going around in circles. "Running off on a hurt paw won't help you find him, even if you *could* run," I said. "You need to stay here so *he* will find *you*. He wouldn't just leave you here hurt, would he?"

Bob was panting now. Lots of dogs pant when they are hurt. Of course it was still hot, and there was no water for him to drink.

"Wait!" I said again. I wasn't even sure if he could hear me now. I gave his nose a lick, and then turned back up the slope to the road.

Dr. Jeanie and the putt-putt were out of sight. I looked up the road. Should I run back to find Carla? I didn't know her well, so I had no idea if she would realize I needed help. Maybe I should wait here for

Dr. Jeanie? No, I should go down
the road, not up. The quicker I went
down, the sooner I would find Dr.
Jeanie.

I set off at a run. It was the right
decision. Soon, I heard the putt-putt's
motor again. It was coming towards
me, and moving faster than before.
I ran on, around one bend, and
another. And there was Dr. Jeanie,
riding back up to meet me.

She looked worried, and cross,
and she called me to come. "Trump,
Trump! There you are! You naughty
dog, why did you jump out?"

I wanted to run to her, but if she
caught me, she would put me into
the dog box and turn back towards
home. I wagged my tail furiously,

but I didn't go to her.

"Trump!" She sounded angry now. "Stop this nonsense!"

I made a little dart up the road, then looked back and wagged my tail again. Dr. Jeanie got off the putt-putt. I did my little dart again, and whined. "This is no time for games. We have to get home for the Clinic!" She frowned.

I turned and ran up the road as fast as I could. Behind me, I heard the putt-putt start up again.

By the time Dr. Jeanie caught up with me, I had almost reached the right place. I waited by the road until I was sure Dr. Jeanie could see me, then I barked twice and darted off down the slope.

The motor stopped, and I heard
Dr. Jeanie call me again. Then I
heard the noise of her boots as she
started down the gully.

I stopped until she came in
sight, then barked. I wished she
could understand me as well as I
understand her. Then I remembered
I am unusual. Even my dad, who

is a very clever dog detective, can only talk to other dogs, although he understands most of what his human says. I wished Dad and Sarge, his person, were here.

By now, Dr. Jeanie must have known I wasn't playing games. Some dogs play running-away games, but I don't do that when I'm on duty. Dr. Jeanie knows that, really.

I hurried on, following my own trail back the short way to where I had left Motorbike Bob. He was still there, lying on his side. He was panting, and I knew he needed help soon. I jumped up and down until I was sure Dr. Jeanie knew where to come, and then I sniffed at Bob.

He opened his eyes when I prodded him with my nose. They looked blurred and dull.

"Dr. Jeanie is coming," I told him. "It's going to be quite all right. She will fix your paw and you'll soon be riding with Greg again." At least, I hoped so!

As soon as Dr. Jeanie saw Bob, she understood why I had run away from her. She gave me a quick ear rub, and then dropped down on her knees to examine Bob.

"Poor old fellow," she said. "Bob, isn't it? You are in a mess, aren't you? What's this then, a nasty gash on your paw? Did you cut that on wire, or broken glass? Or did you do this when you jumped off the bike? We'd better stop that bleeding before we do anything else."

Dr. Jeanie often talks aloud to animals when she's treating them. Sometimes I think she's also telling herself what to do. It's useful, because I learn a lot that way. She pulled a big handkerchief out of her pocket, and tied it firmly around Motorbike Bob's leg as a **tourniquet** to slow the bleeding. He yelped, and tried to pull his paw away.

Tourniquet (TOR-nee-kay) – A band with a stick or something similar twisted into it to make it tight. It helps stop bleeding.

"You're awake, anyway," said

Dr. Jeanie. "We need to get you to Pet Vet right away, but that old bike won't do." She ran her hands over Bob's head and sides and his other legs. "Everything else seems all right, so I'll risk carrying you. Come on, old boy." She put her arms around Bob and got up, lifting him with her. "Lead the way, Trump!"

I trotted up the slope. Dr. Jeanie came after me more slowly. She knew I would guide her back to where we'd left the putt-putt. When we reached the road, Dr. Jeanie stood with Bob in her arms, looking at the dog box.

"That's not big enough for both of you," she said. "We need a real vehicle." She bent and put Bob carefully in a patch of shade by the road. Then she looked down at me. "Trump, you stay with this fellow. Do you understand? Stay. I'll be as quick as I can." She took a bit of twine out of her pocket and tied it through my collar, then fastened it to Bob's collar as well. Next, she took some bandages out of the saddle bag and wrapped it over the handkerchief around Bob's leg.

"Wait!" she said to us, then got back on the putt-putt and drove up the hill.

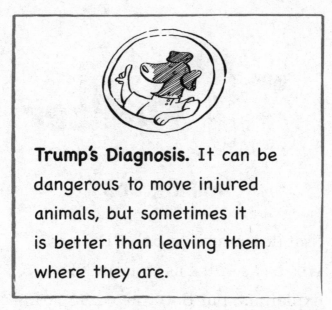

Trump's Diagnosis. It can be
dangerous to move injured
animals, but sometimes it
is better than leaving them
where they are.

Helping Bob

I sat down next to Bob. "Dr. Jeanie
will be as quick as she can," I
explained, but Bob was whimpering
and upset.

"I know your paw hurts," I said.
"When we get to Pet Vet Dr. Jeanie
will give you something to stop it
hurting. Then she'll fix it."

"I have to go to Greg," said Bob.

"Well, you can't. And I can't
either. Dr. Jeanie told me to stay
with you." I didn't point out that we

were both tied up. That might have upset Bob even more. I had a feeling he hadn't been tied up very often in his life. "You'll be all right," I said. "It won't be long before you're running around again."

I lay down with my head on my paws to wait. Bob kept fretting. I just wished Greg would come back

from wherever he had gone. Maybe he could explain to Dr. Jeanie about how Bob had been hurt.

Dr. Jeanie had left us in a patch of shade, but it was still hot. Fortunately, she was back quite soon, riding in a Land Rover with Carla Lother. They both got out, and Carla came to look at Bob.

"It *is* Motorbike Bob," she said. "Poor old boy. This must explain why Greg's so late. Bob must have been hurt and …" Her voice trailed off and she looked around. "Where *is* Greg? He wouldn't just leave Bob."

"I'm sure he wouldn't," agreed Dr. Jeanie. "Maybe Bob ran off or fell off and your brother is looking for him."

"Greg?" yelled Carla. "Greg! Are you there?"

The sound echoed around the gully.

"We can't wait around, Carla," said Dr. Jeanie. "I have to get that paw cleaned and stitched as quickly as possible. He's still losing blood."

"Yes, of course. I'll drive you to Pet Vet, if you hold Bob. What about your dog?"

"Trump will sit near my feet," said Dr. Jeanie.

Once more we started off down the winding road. Carla kept looking from side to side as she drove. She was watching for Greg.

"If he's fallen off his bike we should be able to see him, or it," she said.

"You should call Jeandabah Run from Pet Vet," said Dr. Jeanie. "He may have gone back there, looking for Bob. If not, I suggest you check down on the slope where we found Bob, just in case he's searching down there and didn't hear you call."

Carla turned off into Kane Miller Road, and soon after that we were back at Pet Vet. We expected there to be a lot of patients lined up outside, since we were late for the Clinic, but the doors were unlocked and everything looked normal. As we dashed inside with Motorbike Bob, we found out why. Dr. Max was in the examination room, checking Dodger's sore back.

He looked up. "There you are,

Jeanie," he said quite loudly. "I told these good folks you had an emergency patient. I see you've brought him in."

I don't see how Dr. Max could have known that, but he must have known Dr. Jeanie wouldn't be late without a good reason. He patted Dodger, and lifted him down from the table, then said, "He'll be fine, Cordelia. He should rest for another day or so, and then give him some gentle exercise."

As Dodger and Cordelia Applebloom went out, Dr. Max wiped down the table, and put a clean towel over it. Dr. Jeanie laid Bob down. He was shivering now, despite the heat, so Dr. Jeanie put another towel over him. "It's only his leg," she said to Dr. Max. "No other injuries."

"I'll leave you to it, then," said Dr. Max. "Do you want me to see the patients in the other room?"

"Thanks, Grandpa." Dr. Jeanie gave him a quick smile. Most of the time, she and I can manage perfectly well without help. We are proud of that, but we understand that the patients have to come before our pride.

Dr. Jeanie gave Bob an injection, then set out all her instruments before she undid the bandages on his paw. This was so his leg would be **numb** while she cleaned it up and

> **Numb** (numm) –
> Unable to feel pain.

stitched it. I sat up on my stool in the alcove, so I was level with the table. That way, I was able to **communicate** with Bob without getting in Dr. Jeanie's way.

> **Communicate** (kom-MEW-nee-kate) – Pass information back and forth. Dogs do it by barking, whining or growling, and also by using their tails and ears for body language.

When his leg had gone numb, Dr. Jeanie clipped off the hair on his paw and then cleaned the wound with **antiseptic**. As usual, it made me sneeze. She worked hard and quickly, and soon the bleeding had stopped. Dr. Jeanie gave Bob another injection, to keep the wound from getting infected. Then she put a **sterile** bandage over it.

> **Antiseptic** (ant-ee-SEP-tic) - Medicine that kills bacteria so wounds don't get infected.

When she had finished, she looked at me and smiled. I wagged my tail

> **Sterile** (stair-ile) - Has no germs on it.

as she carried Bob into the recovery ward. Now it was my turn.

It was still very hot, but Dr. Jeanie opened the window to let in some fresh air. Bob had stopped shivering. He was looking around in a dazed sort of way.

"Trump?"

"I'm here," I said. "If you feel
thirsty, there's some water in the
bowl."

"I have to find Greg," said Bob.
He tried to get up, but his leg was
still numb, so he couldn't manage.

"You need to rest," I said. "You're
not well."

"I'm always well. Greg says I'm

the healthiest dog ever!"

"Even healthy dogs need help sometimes. Vets like Dr. Jeanie help dogs like you to go on being healthy."

Bob sighed. "You might be right, but you don't understand. I *have* to get to Greg!"

"I know most of the time you can do anything that needs doing, but sometimes it takes a human to deal with another human. The best thing you can do is to be ready to greet him when he comes for you."

"But he *can't* come," whined Bob. "He's hurt. I was coming to find someone when I cut my paw."

Trump's Diagnosis. Wounds need to be treated properly. If they are bad, they might have to be sewn up. Keeping them clean and dry helps them to heal properly.

Happy Ending

This was not good news. I was on my way to find Dr. Jeanie when the telephone rang. I sat down at her feet to listen.

"I see," said Dr. Jeanie after a bit. "So Greg actually rode down the slope and right into the gully! It's a good thing you found the wheel marks. If he asks about his dog, tell him Bob is all right. It looks as if he cut his paw on broken glass. He might have been trying to get to you, poor fellow. Really, he'll be fine, though he'll have a scar."

Dr. Jeanie hung up the telephone as Dr. Max came in. "That's the last of the Clinic patients," he said. "Quite like old times, it was."

Dr. Jeanie bent to rub my ears.

"I just found out what happened to the border collie's owner," she said to Dr. Max. "It's the strangest thing," said Dr. Jeanie. "After he helped me fix the Ariel —"

"What?" Dr. Max looked worried. "Where *is* the Ariel? What happened to it?"

"It's fine now. I left it at Elias Hill. The chain came off and Greg, the border collie's owner, stopped to help me. Then he headed off to

Carla's place."

"Why would he go there?"

Dr. Jeanie sighed. "He's her brother, and he was going to help her out for a couple of weeks. Anyway, on the way up the hill, according to Carla, he smelled smoke."

"I'm not surprised," said Dr. Max. "People get careless in this hot weather."

"He's the sort of person who *fixes* things, so he rode his bike off the road and down into the gully to see what was burning," said Dr. Jeanie. "Carla says someone had been camping down in the gully. There was some broken glass, and other rubbish, and they hadn't put the fire out properly. Greg put it out, but it seems he slipped and fell on his way back to the bike and hit his head. Poor Bob may have tried to get to him and trodden in that glass."

Dr. Max whistled. "I hope this Greg is not too badly hurt."

"Carla said he was able to call out when she was following the bike tracks. She's taken him to the hospital and they're keeping him in for observation."

"But how did you come to find the dog in the gully?" asked Dr. Max.

"I didn't.

> **Observation**
> (OB-ser-vay-sh"n)
> – In the hospital so doctors can watch and make sure nothing else is wrong.

Trump did. She jumped out of the

dog box on the putt-putt and led me right to him." She rubbed my ears.

So did Dr. Max. "It's as well she did. I'm sure they'd have found the man sooner or later, but I'd say you only just got to the dog in time."

I left them talking. Of course, it was good to hear Dr. Jeanie and Dr. Max saying nice things about me,

but I am an A.L.O. I had a job to do.

I went straight back to Motorbike Bob and told him the good news.

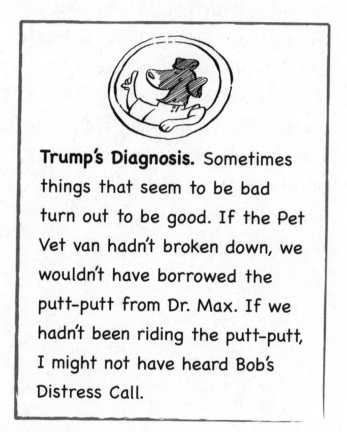

Trump's Diagnosis. Sometimes things that seem to be bad turn out to be good. If the Pet Vet van hadn't broken down, we wouldn't have borrowed the putt-putt from Dr. Max. If we hadn't been riding the putt-putt, I might not have heard Bob's Distress Call.

ABout the Authors

Darrel and Sally Odgers live in
Tasmania with their Jack Russell
terriers, Tess, Trump, Pipwen, Jeanie
and Preacher, who compete to take
them for walks. They enjoy walks,
because that's when they plan their
stories. They toss ideas around and
pick the best. They are also the
authors of the popular Jack Russell:
Dog Detective series.